A Big Deal in Mousetown:
STOOPID CATS book 2

BRENT JACKSON

BENEDICTION

"I'm in no rush, I know where this road goes."

OCCASIONAL TABLE OF DISCONTENTS

ACKNOWLEDGMENTS

There's so many people to thank, so let's not and say we did.

BIRD MID-AIR COLLISIONS
VERY RARE.

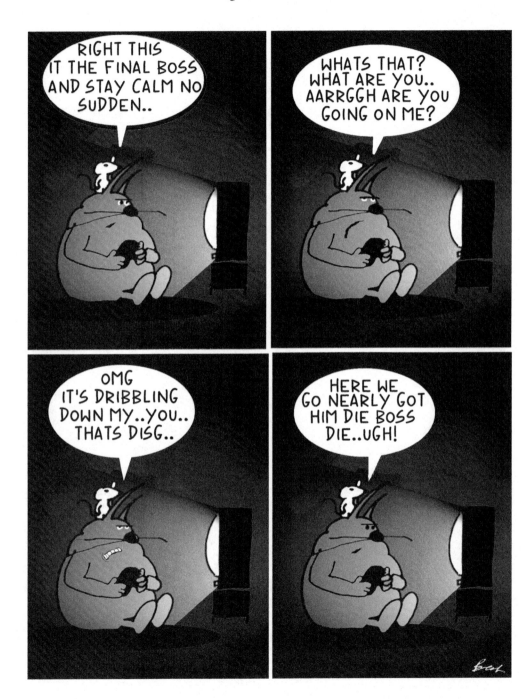

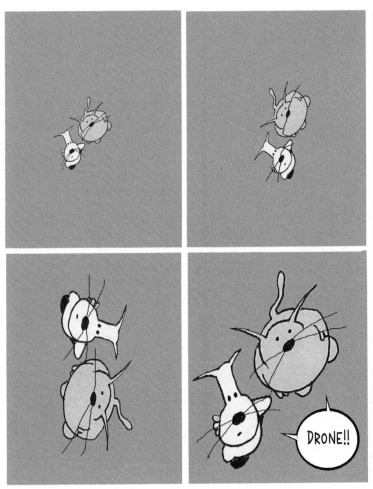

CLOUD GAZING AND THE PECULIARITY OF VISION

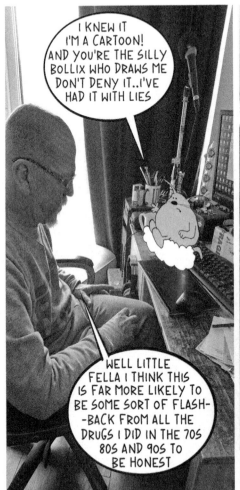

ABOUT THE AUTHOR

Brent Jackson is an iconoclast and in truth he started fully being one when one day, sitting in a tree in Grove Hill, Hemel Hempstead, he found out what that word meant and how to spell it. After that all other words seemed like pale, sickly, pallid, shambling simpletons by comparison and poetry grandeur was only a short space hopper bounce away. As well as being a poet, singer, front man, songsmith, artist and cartoonist, he is a father, a grandfather, a son, a partner, a lover, a friend and a carer. He nurtures his family as if they are plants and his plants as if they were family. He nurtures his friends as though they are hungry zoo animals. There are cats in his life, the current incumbents working their way studiously through their nine lives as the others did before them. At no time have any of them sat in holes and pondered the universe. As far as we know. Also very few of them are cartoons. The ones that are deny it strenuously. Brent lives in Brighton with his family, plants, cats, and many, many, many cartoons.

Printed in Great Britain
by Amazon